My Baby Blue Jays

Photographs and text by **John Berendt**

VIKING

An Imprint of Penguin Group (USA) Inc.

VIKING
Published by Penguin Group
Penguin Young Readers Group, 345 Hudson Street, New York, New York 10014, U.S.A.
Penguin Group (Canada), 90 Eglinton Avenue East, Suite 700, Toronto, Ontario, Canada M4P 2Y3
(a division of Pearson Penguin Canada Inc.)
Penguin Books Ltd, 80 Strand, London WC2R 0RL, England
Penguin Ireland, 25 St Stephen's Green, Dublin 2, Ireland (a division of Penguin Books Ltd)
Penguin Group (Australia), 250 Camberwell Road, Camberwell, Victoria 3124, Australia
(a division of Pearson Australia Group Pty Ltd)
Penguin Books India Pvt Ltd, 11 Community Centre, Panchsheel Park, New Delhi – 110 017, India
Penguin Group (NZ), 67 Apollo Drive, Rosedale, North Shore 0632, New Zealand
(a division of Pearson New Zealand Ltd)
Penguin Books (South Africa) (Pty) Ltd, 24 Sturdee Avenue, Rosebank, Johannesburg 2196, South Africa

Penguin Books Ltd, Registered Offices: 80 Strand, London WC2R 0RL, England

First published in 2011 by Viking, a division of Penguin Young Readers Group

1 3 5 7 9 10 8 6 4 2

LIBRARY OF CONGRESS CATALOGING-IN-PUBLICATION DATA
Berendt, John.
My baby blue jays / by John Berendt.
p. cm.
ISBN 978-0-670-01290-9 (hardcover)
1. Birds I. Title.
QL676.B4694 2011
598.8'64—dc22
2010033296

Manufactured in China • Set in Cochin

Design concept: Carter Hooper

For Henrik and Olivia

I live in a white house on a quiet street in a big city—New York.

There is a small iron balcony just outside the windows of my office, which is on the third floor.

One day, a blue jay landed on the railing of the balcony. It surprised me, because I don't often see birds so close up. The blue jay inspected the balcony very carefully.

Then he flew back to his wife in a nearby tree and they chirped to each other. He must have told her that he'd found a place where they could build a nest. Do you know why I think so?

Because he began making a nest right away. First, he picked up a strip of white plastic that he found in the street and brought it up to the balcony.

And then he and his wife added twigs and grass until the nest was finished. You can even see the original strip of white plastic sticking out at the top.

Very soon Mama blue jay laid an egg in it. In fact, she laid three eggs! Then she stood guard over the eggs, to protect them from cats or squirrels who might come along and steal them. I kept a lookout too.

After a few weeks, three little blue jays were born.

They settled into their new home and were very curious
about anybody, like me, who took a close look at them.

They did a lot of chirping and cheeping. Papa blue jay came back to the nest to see what all the fuss was about. Aha! He knew! The little ones were hungry!

So he fed them by putting food into their mouths right from his own mouth. That's just how birds do it. And what do you think he gave them to eat? Bugs and worms!

After a few weeks, it was time for the baby blue jays to leave the nest and go out on their own. To run around. To hop. And best of all, maybe, to fly! At last one of the little birds hopped out of the nest.

When the other two saw him standing out there on the balcony, they cheered him on. They, too, were eager to hop out of the nest.

And they did! Before long, all three birds were hopping around on the balcony. They practiced flying by flapping their wings. But mostly they hopped, because they weren't strong enough to fly. Not yet anyway.

Soon it was time to get off the balcony and onto the ground, but this was a big step, because the balcony is on the third floor of my house. There is quite a long drop to the ground.

One of the birds looked at me as if to say, "Well, it's been swell here, but I'm afraid it's time for me to go." He looked a little nervous, I thought.

But he gathered up his courage and squeezed between two of the bars and out into the air. As he fell, he fluttered his wings frantically. Not enough to fly, just enough to slow his fall a little. He landed with a thump—not a bad one, though—and he found himself on the doormat in front of my house. Being a cautious fellow, he looked first to the left and then to the right.

Then he took one last look back up at the nest. And without further ado, he stepped off the mat onto the brick courtyard and hopefully into the big wide world.

But first he would have to make his way up a few steps to get to the street! He still couldn't really fly, and his hopping wasn't going to raise him high enough to get up the steps. What should he do?

He thought about it for a while.

And then he did two things at once: he hopped *and* he fluttered his wings.

And it worked! That was one step done.

Almost to the gate!

At last he reached the top step. And he looked out through the gate at the sidewalk. Once again, he looked first to his left. And then to his right.

And then he took his first step out onto 87th Street!

Now his biggest worry was getting stepped on by people who didn't see him. So, very quickly, he hopped and fluttered across the sidewalk to the curb. It was much safer there.

Okay. Now that he was at the curb where the parked cars were,
he thought he'd take a little walk with rest stops in between.
Finally he saw a nice spot for a pleasant rest!

He hopped onto a wooden fence around a small garden at the base of a tree a few houses up the block from mine. He was enchanted by a pretty pink flower. He'd never seen anything like it before.

And he took a breather, because his first walk had been a strenuous one.

Nobody would make the mistake of stepping on him here.

I thought I saw a little smile of satisfaction on his face. Do you?

Later that day, he came back to my moss garden to say good-bye. I told him I would miss him, but I would always remember him and his brothers—or his sisters—because to tell you the truth I couldn't tell which birds were girls and which were boys. But I did know that the big bird who laid the eggs had to be the mama.

Now the blue jay is all grown up. I'm sure I've seen him around the neighborhood, but by now he looks so much like the other grown-up blue jays that I'm not sure which he is. He's probably one of the birds who fly into my backyard once in a while and take baths in my fountain—like this one.